To my husband, Steve, and my daughters, Lily and Laurel, who make everything the best story.

And to Lorin and Carole Zissman for their time, love, and support.

www.mascotbooks.com

Santa's Puppies!

©2017 Sherry Ann Brescia. All Rights Reserved. No part of this publication may be reproduced, stored in a retrieval system or transmitted in any form by any means electronic, mechanical, or photocopying, recording or otherwise without the permission of the author.

For more information, please contact:
Mascot Books
560 Herndon Parkway #120
Herndon, VA 20170
info@mascotbooks.com

Library of Congress Control Number: 2017908676

CPSIA Code: PRT0917A
ISBN-13: 978-1-68401-160-5

Printed in the United States

Santa's Puppies

by Sherry Ann Brescia

Illustrated by
Vanessa Alexandre

Rosy was an abandoned dog who dreamed of finding a family.

She lived in the forest with her outdoor friends, where she wandered day after day searching for her forever home.

One night, Rosy couldn't sleep. Her stomach had gotten so big it almost touched the ground. She was going to become a mommy this special night!

Rosy was trying to rest when she heard the sound of jingling bells. Was someone coming to rescue her just in the nick of time? She followed the sound to the edge of the forest.

There she found a sleigh with soft velvet lining and lots of presents. It looked like a cozy place to rest. Rosy introduced herself to the reindeer, and they invited her to hide within the presents.

As soon as Rosy was comfortably snuggled in, the sleigh took off! It was flying! *It's a miracle*, she thought. But then the real miracle happened.

Rosy had her babies right in Santa's sleigh! And because they were born in Santa's sleigh, each was blessed with Santa's magical spirit.

Rosy wondered what to do now. Her puppies didn't have homes either.

Then Rosy noticed Santa giving his presents to good girls and boys, and she knew what she had to do.

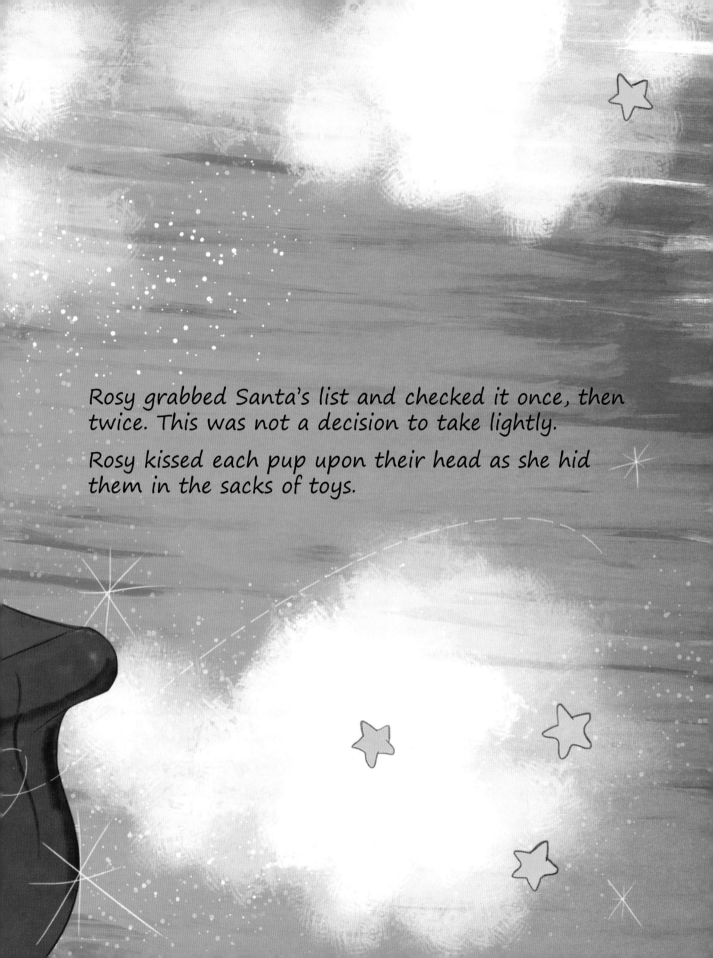

Rosy grabbed Santa's list and checked it once, then twice. This was not a decision to take lightly.

Rosy kissed each pup upon their head as she hid them in the sacks of toys.

One by one, Santa took a pup-filled sack and flew down the chimney until all of them had been delivered.

When Santa returned to the North Pole, he was surprised to find Rosy in his empty sleigh. He brought her out of the cold and into Mrs. Claus's warm arms.

As soon as Mrs. Claus and Rosy saw each other, they fell in love! Santa realized it was the best present he had ever given Mrs. Claus.

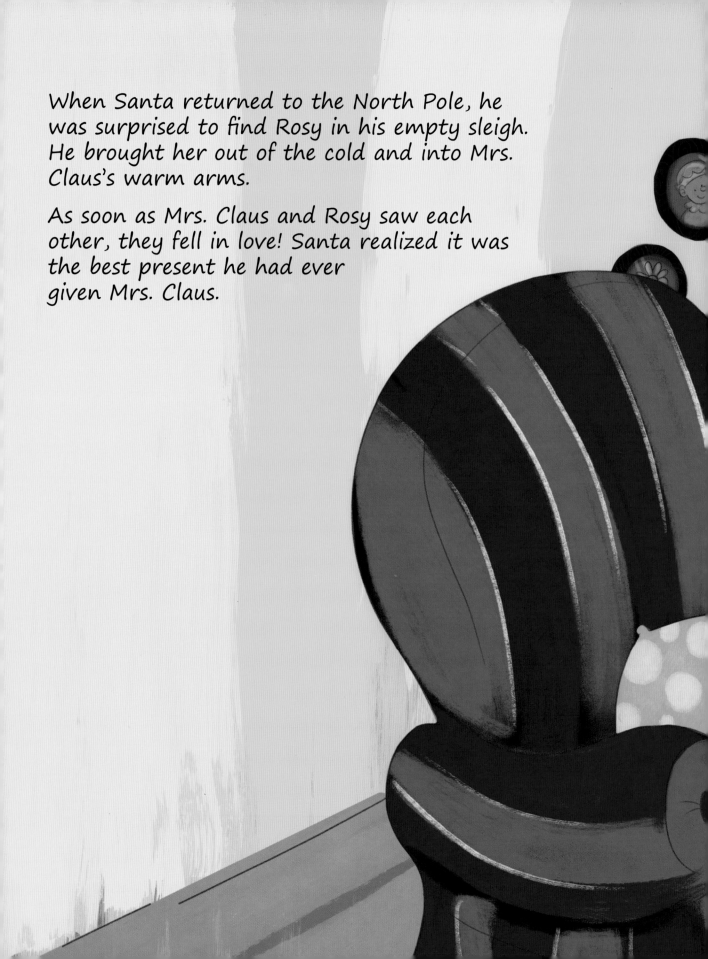

On Christmas morning, the Claus family gathered around the TV. To their surprise, the headline story was Santa's puppies!

But Santa knew the truth. Rosy had saved her puppies by gifting them to the world.

Rosy looked around. She had found her forever home.

Still, she remembered her friends waiting to be rescued. So the next time she met a pup without a home, she brought it to Santa's workshop. And Santa knew what he had to do.

He and Mrs. Claus opened a rescue shelter where all puppies and dogs without a home were welcomed.

And every Christmas Eve, Rosy rode in the sleigh with Santa and chose the right forever home for these dogs.

Rosy made sure each child was loving and responsible. Only those with the biggest hearts made it onto Rosy's extra-special list.

Soon, good girls and boys all over the world started wishing for Santa's puppies instead of toys. A waiting list grew. Santa and the elves wondered what to do.

And then a cat wandered into *Santa's* hat...

Have a book idea?

Contact us at:

info@mascotbooks.com | www.mascotbooks.com